BOOK 2 • Clarinet

BEST IN CLASS

Dear Student,

Welcome to **BEST IN CLASS, BOOK 2!**

With the skills you are mastering on your instrument, I am sure you are beginning to see how music can add new dimensions to your life.

As you continue to study, you will quickly see that with more proficiency on your instrument comes a greater experience of the beauty and joy of music.

To play your instrument well, careful practice is essential. You will find a chart below to help you keep track of your practice time. Always strive to do your best.

Best wishes in reaching your musical goals!

Bruce Pearson

PRACTICE RECORD CHART

WEEK	DAY 1	DAY 2	DAY 3	DAY 4	DAY 5	DAY 6	DAY 7	TOTAL TIME	PARENT'S INITIALS	WEEKLY GRADE
1										
2										
3										
4										
5										
6										
7										
8										
9										
10										
11										
12										
13										
14										
15										
16										
17										
18										

WEEK	DAY 1	DAY 2	DAY 3	DAY 4	DAY 5	DAY 6	DAY 7	TOTAL TIME	PARENT'S INITIALS	WEEKLY GRADE
19										
20										
21										
22										
23										
24										
25										
26										
27										
28										
29										
30										
31										
32										
33										
34										
35										
36										

W4CL

ISBN   0-8497-5876-9

DAILY WARM-UPS . . . for clarinets only

A. STEADY TONE

★ Always play with your best tone. Keep your tone steady.
1. Play each note *p* ⟨ *f* ⟩ *p*
2. Play each note with the following articulation pattern: ♩ ♩ ♫♫♫♫ . Strive for a clean attack on each note.

B. SMOOTH SLURS

★Keep your embouchure firm and your air stream steady.

C. CROSSING THE BREAK

★Hold your right hand down for the entire line.

D. PHRASES, PHRASES

Andante

mf ★Can you play this line in one breath?

E. BOTTOM TO TOP

Moderato

mf

1st time — slur   2nd time — play legato

1. MOVING CHORDS

Band Arrangement

2. TECHNIC TRAINER

3. C MAJOR (B♭ Concert) SCALE, THIRDS, AND ARPEGGIOS

★ Write in the note names before you play.

4. THEME FROM "PRINCE IGOR"
Moderato

Alexander Borodin

mf ★ Write in a breath mark at the end of each phrase.

5. KOOKABURRA
Allegro

4-Part Round

6. TECHNIC TRAINER Moderato

7. DANCE FROM "ORPHEUS AND EURYDICE"
Andante

Christoph Gluck

★Be sure to keep your fingers close to the keys.

8. A MINOR (G minor Concert) SCALE
Andante

9. DOWN BY THE RIVER
Andante

Traditional

10. RHYTHM RAMBLES
1. Draw in the bar lines.   2. Write in the counting.   3. Clap the rhythm before you play.

SOMETHING SPECIAL . . . for clarinets only
alternate

★Use the alternate F fingering.

NEW NOTES

NEW NOTE

NEW NOTE

THEORY GAME

SPECIAL EXERCISE

NEW NOTE

★ W4CL

NEW IDEA

NEW IDEA

THEORY GAMES

| ACCENT | | Play the note with the accent (>) a little louder. |

11. LITTLE BROWN JUG

Joe Winner

| EIGHTH REST | γ = 1/2 beat of silence

An eighth rest is half as long as a quarter rest. | 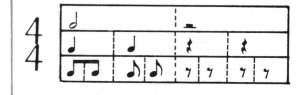 |

1. Before you play exercises 12 through 16, write in the counting. 2. Then clap and count the rhythm.

12. REST ON THREE

13. REST ON TWO

14. REST ON FOUR

15. REST OFF THE BEAT

16. REST ON THE BEAT

17. THE GOOD KING HAS RHYTHM

Moderato

SPECIAL EXERCISE

SOMETHING SPECIAL . . . for clarinets only

NEW NOTES W4CL

1st time — play the lower notes   2nd time — play the upper notes

NEW IDEA

| SYNCOPATION | 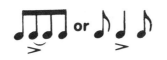 | Play an accent on a note that is normally not a strong pulse. |

18. PLAY IT STRONG

★ Write in the counting before you play.

NEW NOTE

19. SHOO-FLY

Moderato

Frank Campbell

20. NOBODY KNOWS THE TROUBLE I'VE SEEN

Andante

Spiritual

21. LIZA JANE

Afro-American Folk Song

Allegro

22. A LATIN LUNCH

Root/Pearson — Band Arrangement

Moderato

1st time - mf   2nd time - f

| LONG REST |  | Rest for the number of measures that are indicated. |

NEW IDEA

23. HOW LONG IS YOUR REST?

Count: 1,2 — 2,2

SPECIAL EXERCISE

SOMETHING SPECIAL . . . for clarinets only

NEW NOTES

lower upper   1st time - play the lower notes   2nd time - play the upper notes

★ These two notes are enharmonic.

W4CL

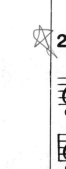

| ONE MEASURE REPEAT | 𝄎 | Repeat the previous measure. |

24. THE TENDERFOOT POLKA

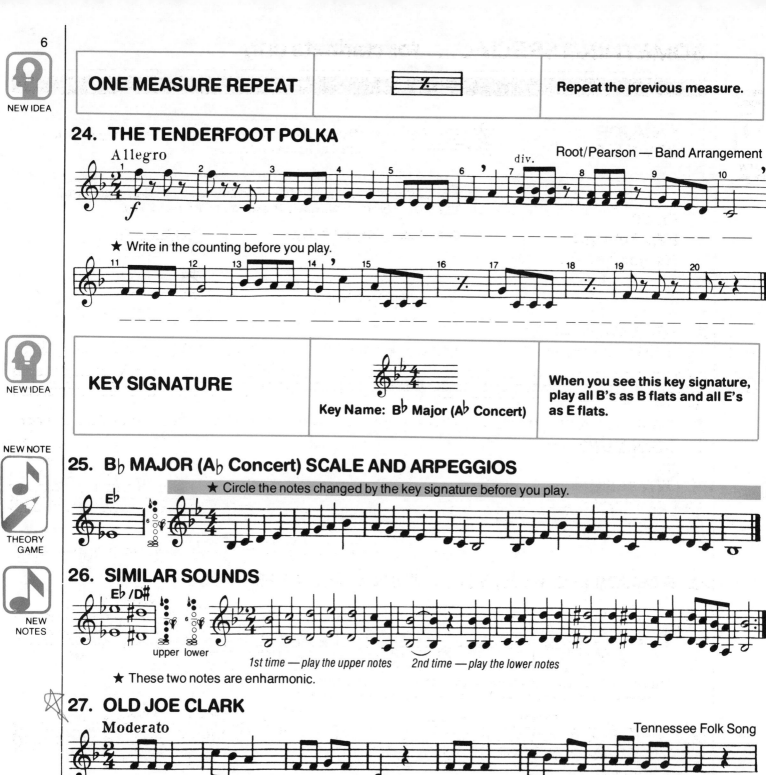

★ Write in the counting before you play.

| KEY SIGNATURE | | When you see this key signature, play all B's as B flats and all E's as E flats. |

Key Name: Bb Major (Ab Concert)

25. Bb MAJOR (Ab Concert) SCALE AND ARPEGGIOS

★ Circle the notes changed by the key signature before you play.

26. SIMILAR SOUNDS

upper lower

1st time — play the upper notes   2nd time — play the lower notes

★ These two notes are enharmonic.

27. OLD JOE CLARK

Moderato — Tennessee Folk Song

28. CHROMATIC CAPERS

enharmonic
enharmonic

★ Use the chromatic Gb fingering.

29. ENHARMONIC HOP

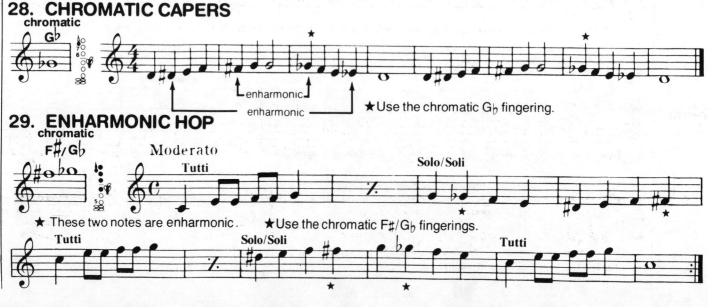

★ These two notes are enharmonic.   ★ Use the chromatic F#/Gb fingerings.

SOMETHING SPECIAL . . . for clarinets only

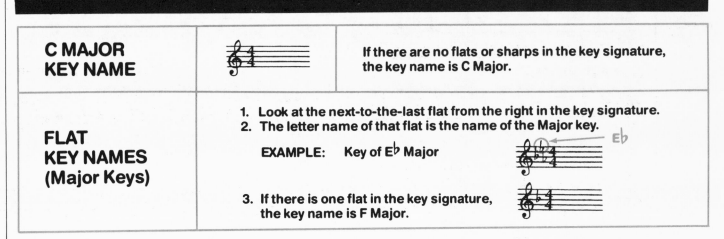

C MAJOR KEY NAME		If there are no flats or sharps in the key signature, the key name is C Major.
FLAT KEY NAMES (Major Keys)	1. Look at the next-to-the-last flat from the right in the key signature. 2. The letter name of that flat is the name of the Major key. EXAMPLE: Key of E♭ Major 3. If there is one flat in the key signature, the key name is F Major.	

A. KEY NAME GAME

★ Write in the key name for each key signature.

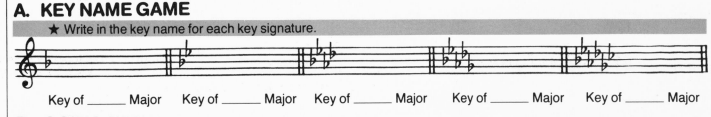

Key of _____ Major   Key of _____ Major   Key of _____ Major   Key of _____ Major   Key of _____ Major

B. GOING UP?

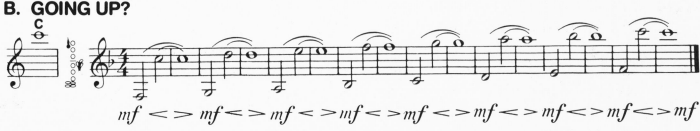

$mf \;<\;> \; mf \;<\;> \; mf \;<\;> \; mf \;<\;> \; mf \;<\;> \; mf \;<\;> \; mf \;<\;> \; mf \;<\;> \; mf$

C. G MAJOR (F Concert) SCALE, THIRDS, AND ARPEGGIOS

1st time — play the lower notes slurred   2nd time — play the upper notes slurred
3rd time — play the lower notes legato   4th time — play the upper notes legato

D. CROSSING THE BREAK

1. Play each measure 4 times.   2. Hold your right hand down for the first three measures.

E. TECHNIC TRAINER

★Use the chromatic F♯ fingering.

★Use the chromatic B♭ fingering.

★Use the chromatic F♯ fingering.

THEORY GAME

30. KEY SIGNATURE CRAZE

★ Circle the notes changed by each key signature before you play.

A.

B.

1st time - play the lower notes   2nd time - play the upper notes

THEORY GAME

31. SONATINA

Ludwig van Beethoven

★ What is the key name for **SONATINA**? _____

Moderato

p

mf

p

NEW IDEA

TIME SIGNATURE	¢ = 2 beats in each measure (ALLA BREVE or CUT TIME)	o = 2 beats = ▬ ♩ = 1 beat = ▬ ♪ = 1/2 beat = 𝄾	¢

32. CUT TIME

★ Write in the counting before you play.

NEW NOTE

33. OATS AND BEANS

American Folk Song

div.

34. OH, SUSANNA

Stephen Foster

★ Write in the counting before you play.

NEW NOTE

35. STARS AND STRIPES FOREVER

John Philip Sousa

Moderato

1.

2.

SPECIAL EXERCISE

SOMETHING SPECIAL . . . for clarinets only

alternate

Andante

mf   ★ Use the alternate C fingering.

NEW NOTE

W4CL

NEW NOTE
THEORY GAME

36. MARK TIME MARCH
Root/Pearson — Band Arrangement

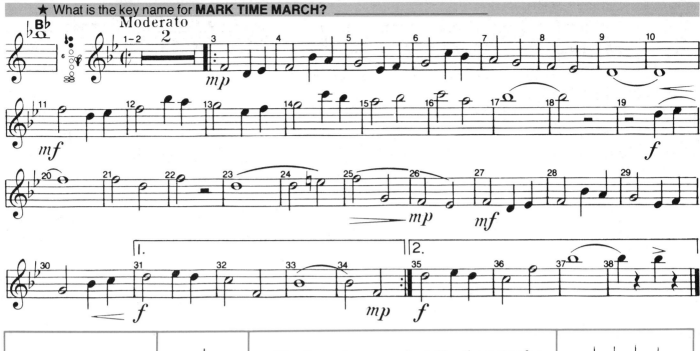

NEW IDEAS

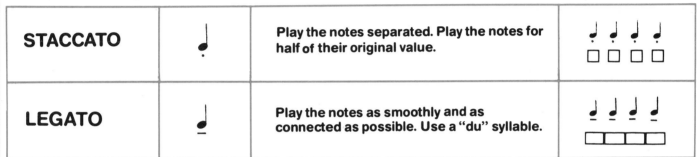

| STACCATO | ♩ | Play the notes separated. Play the notes for half of their original value. | |
| LEGATO | ♩ | Play the notes as smoothly and as connected as possible. Use a "du" syllable. | |

37. STACCATO AND LEGATO

★ Separate the staccato notes and sustain the legato notes.

38. THEME FROM "SURPRISE SYMPHONY"
Franz Joseph Haydn

NEW IDEA

| SIMILE | simile (sim.) | Continue in the same way. |

39. TECHNIC TRAINER

★ How's your wind speed?

SOMETHING SPECIAL . . . for clarinets only

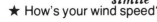

L = use your left hand little finger   R = use your right hand little finger

SPECIAL EXERCISE

W4CL

NEW IDEA

| D.S. AL FINE | D. S. (del segno) = sign
Fine = finish | When you see the *D. S. al Fine*, go back to the 𝄋 (sign) and stop when you come to the *Fine*. |

40. THE ASH GROVE

Old Welsh Air

THEORY GAME

41. CRIPPLE CREEK

Traditional

★ Write in the note names before you play.

42. TECHNIC TRAINER

★ Constant air and quick fingers will make this easier!

43. LITTLE DANCE

★ Write in the counting before you play.

SOMETHING SPECIAL . . . for clarinets only

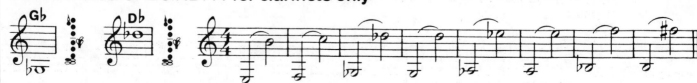

NEW NOTES

44. THE HIGH SCHOOL CADETS MARCH

John Philip Sousa

45. MARACAS GO UP AND DOWN

Mexican Folk Song

★Keep your fingers close to the keys.

| SIXTEENTH NOTE | ♬ = 1/4 beat A sixteenth note is half as long as an eighth note. | 2/4 |

46. RHYTHM MIX

Moderato

★ Write in the counting before you play.

47. OLD BRASS WAGON

Moderato

Southern Tune

48. JING-A-LING

American Camp Song

49. STEADY AS YOU GO

★ What is the key name for **STEADY AS YOU GO?** _____

1st time — *play the upper notes*   2nd time — *play the lower notes*

50. TECHNIC TRAINER

SOMETHING SPECIAL . . . for clarinets only

alternate   Moderato

★Use the alternate B♭ fingering.

W4CL

NEW IDEA

THEORY GAME

SPECIAL EXERCISE

NEW NOTE

SOMETHING SPECIAL . . . for clarinets only

SHARP KEY NAMES (Major Keys)

1. Look at the last sharp to the right in the key signature.
2. The letter name of the next line or space above is the name of the Major key.

   EXAMPLE: Key of D Major

3. If there are six sharps in the key signature, the key name is F♯ Major.

4. If there are seven sharps in the key signature, the key name is C♯ Major.

A. KEY NAME GAME

★ Write in the key name for each key signature.

Key of _____ Major   Key of _____ Major   Key of _____ Major   Key of _____ Major   Key of _____ Major

B. SMOOTH SLURS

★Are you playing with a constant air stream?

C. B♭ MAJOR (A♭ Concert) SCALE, THIRDS, AND ARPEGGIOS

1st time — play the lower notes slurred   2nd time — play the upper notes slurred
3rd time — play the lower notes legato   4th time — play the upper notes legato

D. TECHNIC TRAINER

★Hold your right hand down for the entire line.

E. CHROMATIC SCALE

W4CL

THEORY GAME

57. MARIANNI

Italian Folk Song

★ What is the form of **MARIANNI**? _____

58. MOVIN' ON UP

59. THE RIDDLE SONG

American Folk Song

THEORY GAME

60. TECHNIC TRAINER

★ What is the key name for **TECHNIC TRAINER**? _____

61. IRISH JIG

Irish Folk Song

1st time — *play the upper notes*   2nd time — *play the lower notes*

62. MUSETTE

Johann Sebastian Bach

1st time — *play the upper notes*   2nd time — *play the lower notes*

63. CAN YOU GUESS MY NAME?

★ Write in the counting before you play.

SOMETHING SPECIAL . . . for clarinets only

Moderato

R   L   R   R L R   L R

64. ARTICULATION ANTICS

Moderato

1st time — play the upper notes   *2nd time — play the lower notes*

TIME SIGNATURE

$\frac{6}{8}$ 6 = 6 beats in each measure
8 = ♪ receives 1 beat

♩. = 6 beats = ▬
♩. = 3 beats = 𝄽.
♩ = 2 beats = 𝄽
♪ = 1 beat = 𝄾

65. COUNT ON IT   *1st time — play the upper notes*   *2nd time — play the lower notes*

1. Count out loud and write in the counting before you play.   2. Clap the rhythm before you play.

66. THE BEAT GOES ON

★ Did you feel 6 beats in each ♩. ?

67. THREE IN ONE

★ Feel 3 beats in each ♩. .

68. TWO IS BETTER THAN ONE

★ Be sure to give the ♩ 2 beats.

69. OFF AND ON

70. FIDDLE-DEE-DEE

English Folk Song

Allegro

f

SOMETHING SPECIAL . . . for clarinets only

Andante

f   L   R   L   R

W4CL

NEW IDEA

SPECIAL EXERCISE

NEW IDEA

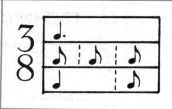

| TIME SIGNATURE | $\mathbf{3}$ = 3 beats in each measure
 $\mathbf{8}$ = ♪ receives 1 beat | ♩. = 3 beats = 𝄽
 ♩ = 2 beats = 𝄾
 ♪ = 1 beat = 𝄿 | |

71. DUET FOR HAND CLAPPERS AND KNEE SLAPPERS

Hand Clappers

Knee Slappers

72. TECHNIC TRAINER

★ Write in the counting and clap the rhythm before you play.

NEW IDEA

| D.S. AL CODA | *D.S. (del segno)* = sign
 al Coda = to Coda | When you see the *D. S. al Coda* go back to the 𝄋 (sign).
 When you come to the ⊕ (Coda sign), skip to the Coda. |

73. BACK TO THE 50'S

Moderato

Root/Pearson — Band Arrangement

SOMETHING SPECIAL . . . for clarinets only

Moderato

SPECIAL EXERCISE
W4CL

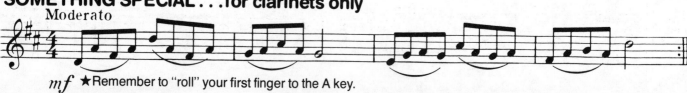

mf ★Remember to "roll" your first finger to the A key.

74. TECHNIC TRAINER

★Be sure to keep your fingers close to the keys.

75. EIGHTH NOTES AND RESTS

A.

B.

C.

D.

E.

Franz Joseph Haydn

76. GERMAN DANCE

THEORY
GAME

★ What is the key name for **GERMAN DANCE?** _____

Moderato

mp

77. VIVE LA COMPAGNIE

French Folk Song

Solo/Soli   Tutti   div.   Solo/Soli

mp   *mf*   *mp*

div. Tutti   Solo/Soli   div. Tutti

f

SOMETHING SPECIAL . . . for clarinets only

SPECIAL
EXERCISE

Andante

mf R   L   R   L   R   L

W4CL

NEW IDEA

| DYNAMICS | ff = *fortissimo* | Play with a very loud volume. |
| | pp = *pianissimo* | Play with a very soft volume. |

MAGIC MOUNTAIN

W4CL

84. THE HUNTING HORN

Allegro

4-Part Round

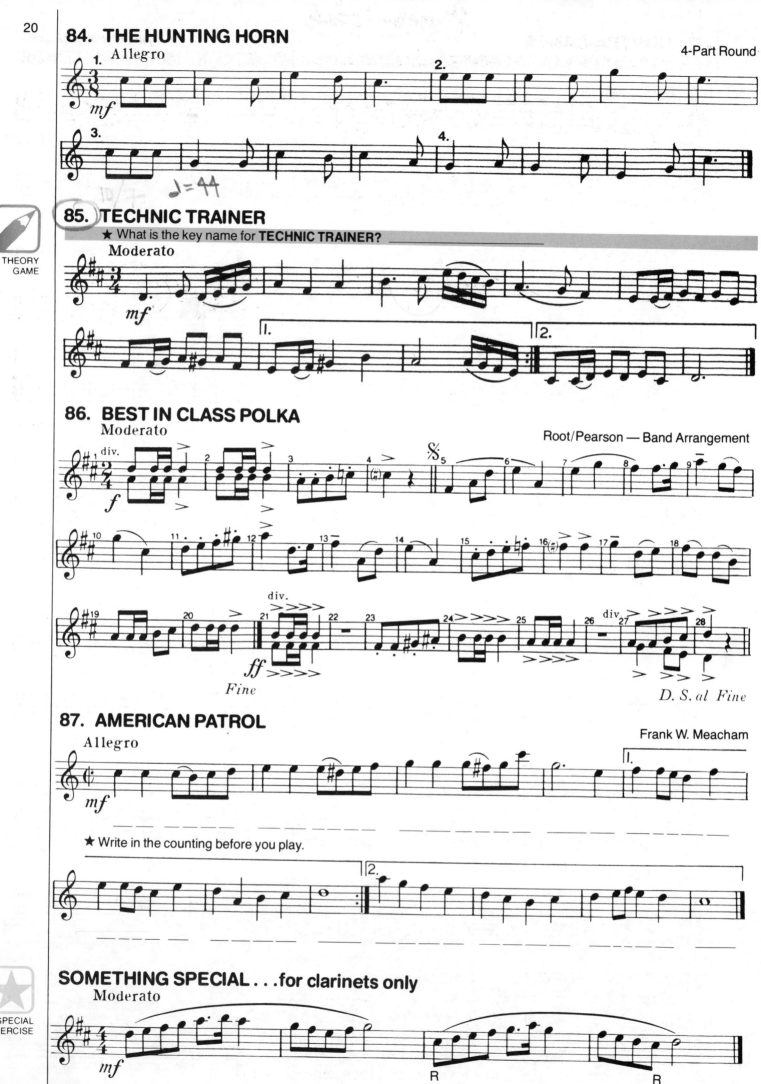

85. TECHNIC TRAINER

★ What is the key name for **TECHNIC TRAINER?** _____

Moderato

86. BEST IN CLASS POLKA

Moderato

Root/Pearson — Band Arrangement

Fine

D. S. al Fine

87. AMERICAN PATROL

Allegro

Frank W. Meacham

★ Write in the counting before you play.

SOMETHING SPECIAL . . .for clarinets only

Moderato

THEORY
GAME

SPECIAL
EXERCISE

W4CL

THEORY GAME

88. CONTRA-DANSE

Wolfgang Amadeus Mozart

★ What is the form of **CONTRA-DANSE**? _____

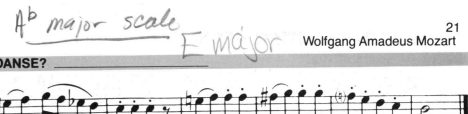

Ab major scale *E major*

89. MARCH OF THE KINGS

Georges Bizet

90. RANGE DEVELOPER

91. TECHNIC TRAINER

92. SKIP TO MY LOU

American Folk Song

★ Tonguing is easier when you use a continuous air stream.

NEW NOTES

SOMETHING SPECIAL . . . for clarinets only

★ "Roll" your left hand first finger off the key for C♯/D♭.

★ These two notes are enharmonic.

W4CL

93. EL CAPITAN MARCH

Allegro

John Philip Sousa

94. CAN YOU COUNT IT?

Moderato

★ Write in the counting before you play.

| KEY SIGNATURE | | When you see this key signature, play all B's as B flats, all E's as E flats, and all A's as A flats. |

Key Name: E♭ Major (D♭ Concert)

95. E♭ MAJOR (D♭ Concert) SCALE, THIRDS, AND ARPEGGIOS

★ Circle the notes that are changed by the key signature before you play.

96. ALOUETTE

French Traditional Song

Tutti

Solo/Soli

Tutti

Solo/Soli   Tutti   Solo/Soli   Tutti   Solo/Soli   Tutti

SOMETHING SPECIAL . . . for clarinets only

Andante

★ "Roll" your left hand first finger off the key for D.

NEW IDEA

THEORY GAME

SPECIAL EXERCISE

NEW NOTE

W4CL

SOMETHING SPECIAL . . . for clarinets only

SPECIAL EXERCISES

A. PHRASE STRETCHER

Moderato

mf ★ Keep the air stream even as you change notes.

B. D MAJOR (C Concert) SCALE, THIRDS, AND ARPEGGIOS

1st time — slur   2nd time — play legato

1st time — play the lower notes slurred   2nd time — play the upper notes slurred
3rd time — play the lower notes legato   4th time — play the upper notes legato

C. TECHNIC TRAINER

★ Play each measure 4 times.

D. TONGUING TRAINER

simile

★ Continue this pattern on the following notes:

K — use Chromatic Fingering

E. CHROMATIC SCALE

W4CL

Page 24

97. DOWN BY THE STATION
★ What is the key name for **DOWN BY THE STATION?** _____

Moderato — 2-Part Round

 NEW IDEA

| TRIPLET |  (triplet) | Each note receives 1/3 of a beat. |

98. TRIPLETS, TRIPLETS, AND MORE TRIPLETS

★ Write in the counting before you play.

99. PILGRIMS' CHORUS

Richard Wagner

 NEW NOTES

100. CHROMATIC CAPERS

★Use the chromatic F♯/G♭ fingerings.

★ Play this exercise again using each of the following articulations:

SOMETHING SPECIAL . . .for clarinets only

Andante

 SPECIAL EXERCISE

★Be sure to use the chromatic E♭ fingering:

W4CL

101. ROLLIN' ROCK

Root/Pearson — Band Arrangement

102. TECHNIC TRAINER

103. OUT FOR THE COUNT

★Write in the counting before you play.

SOMETHING SPECIAL . . . for clarinets only

104. CAN-CAN

Jacques Offenbach

Allegro

105. TONGUING TRAINER

Moderato

★ Write in the counting before you play.

106. MARCH FROM "NUTCRACKER SUITE"

Peter Ilyich Tchaikovsky

Moderato

107. TECHNIC TRAINER

Andante

SOMETHING SPECIAL . . .for clarinets only

Moderato

108. CHROMATIC SCALE

★ Memorize this scale.

1st time — play the lower notes   *2nd time — play the upper notes*

109. ARKANSAS TRAVELER

Folk Song

Moderato

mf

opt.

opt.

110. FATHER OF VICTORY

L. Ganne

f ★Are you playing with a constant air stream and a good hand position?

111. CAN YOU COUNT IT?

Fine

★ Write in the counting before you play.

D. C. al Fine

SIXTEENTH REST

♪ = 1/4 beat of silence

A sixteenth rest is half as long as an eighth rest.

112. SIXTEENTH STUDY

1. On each of the following exercises, write in the counting before you play. 2. Play each exercise 4 times.

A.

B.

C.

D.

NEW IDEA

THEORY GAME

W4CL

113. THE GLENDY BURK

Stephen Foster

Moderato

★ Write in the counting before you play.

10/19/95

114. RULE BRITANNIA

F# major scale also.

Moderato

English Folk Song

mf

f

rit.

115. THEME FROM "SWAN LAKE"

Andante

Peter Ilyich Tchaikovsky

p

★ Write in a breath mark at the end of each phrase.

Fine

mf *p*

f *rit.*

D. C. al Fine

116. TECHNIC TRAINER

★ What is the key name for **TECHNIC TRAINER?** _____

Allegro

THEORY
GAME

SPECIAL
EXERCISE

SOMETHING SPECIAL . . . for clarinets only

Eb /D#

Andante

NEW
NOTES

mf

★ These two notes are enharmonic.

W4CL

SOMETHING SPECIAL . . .for clarinets only

A. ROLL THAT FINGER

1. "Roll" your left hand first finger off the key for the upper notes.   2. Don't forget to use the Eb key for high D.

B. Eb MAJOR (Db Concert) SCALE, THIRDS, AND ARPEGGIOS

1st time — slur   2nd time — play legato

1st time — play the lower notes slurred   2nd time — play the upper notes slurred
3rd time — play the lower notes legato   4th time — play the upper notes legato

C. TECHNIC TRAINER

★Play each measure 4 times.

★Use the 3 key for Eb.   ★Use the 3 key for Bb.   ★Use the 6 key for Eb.   ★Use the 6 key for Bb.

alternate

★Use the alternate Eb fingering.

★Use the alternate Bb fingering:

D. CHROMATIC SCALE

1st time — slur   2nd time — play legato

W4CL

117. MARCH FROM "AIDA"

Giuseppe Verdi

Moderato

118. OUR DIRECTOR MARCH

F.E. Bigelow

Moderato

Solo
Duet

Trio

119. BATTLE HYMN OF THE REPUBLIC

William Steffe

★ What is the key name for **BATTLE HYMN OF THE REPUBLIC?**

Andante

THEORY
GAME

12/20/96

W4CL

120. MARCH FOR DEE

Root/Pearson — Band Arrangement

play 2nd time only

D. S. al Coda

W4CL

SCALE STUDIES

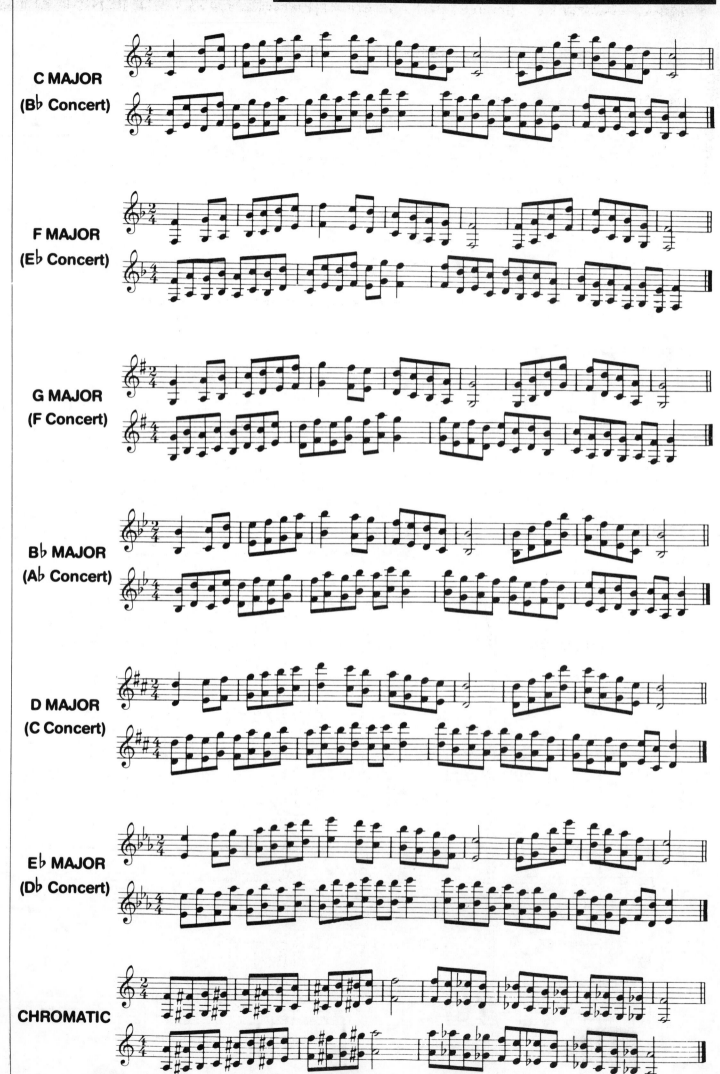